THE MUSEUM OF CONTRADICTIONS

THE MUSEUM OF CONTRADICTIONS

ANTOINE WAUTERS

Translated from the French by
STEPHANIE SMEE

SELKIES HOUSE
LIMITED

INVERNESS

Originally published in France by Éditions du sous-sol
as *Le musée des contradictions* in 2022

First published in the UK in 2025

by

Selkies House Limited
registered at:
Elm House,
Cradlehall Business Park,
Inverness, IV2 5GH

www.selkieshouse.com

9 8 7 6 5 4 3 2 1

Copyright © Antoine Wauters, 2022
Translation copyright © 2025, Stephanie Smee

The moral right of Antoine Wauters to be recognised as the author of this work has been asserted in accordance with the Copyright, Designs and Patents Act, 1988.

Stephanie Smee asserts her moral right to be recognised
as the translator of the work.

"The Game is Over" by Ingeborg Bachmann: Anrufung des Großen Bären
© Piper Verlag GmbH, München 2011

All rights reserved. No part of this publication may be reproduced
or transmitted in any form or by any means, electronic or mechanical,
including photocopy, recording, or any information storage
and retrieval system, without permission in writing from the publisher.
A CIP catalogue record for this book is available from
the British Library

ISBN Paperback 9781917254229
ISBN eBook 9781917254236
ISBN Audiobook 9781917254243

Typeset in Adobe Caslon Pro by Carol Wombly @ Adobe Fonts.
Printed and bound in Great Britain by TJ Books, Padstow, PL28 8RW.

Contents

1. Regarding the forbidden sea	*9*
2. Regarding a troop of pyjama-clad escapees	*17*
3. Regarding the castle in ashes	*27*
4. Regarding paradise	*35*
5. Regarding that place beyond the Wall	*43*
6. Regarding the cement mixers	*51*
7. Regarding a diminished country	*61*
8. Regarding the great sequoia	*69*
9. Regarding the minority who became the majority	*77*
10. Regarding a pain with no name	*87*
11. Regarding a recovered distant joy	*95*
12. Regarding some questions	*103*
Principal guides to the museum	*111*
Translator's note	*113*

... the test of a first-rate intelligence is the ability to hold two opposed ideas in the mind at the same time, and and still retain the ability to function. One should, for example, be able to see that things are hopeless and yet be determined to make them otherwise.

F. Scott Fitzgerald
"The Crack-Up"

What were the hippies of '66-'67 saying with the inarticulate language that was the monolithic sign of hair?
They were saying this: "We are fed up with this culture of consumerism. Our protest is radical. We are creating an antibody to that culture through refusal."

Pier Paolo Pasolini
"Il discorso dei capelli"

I

Regarding the forbidden sea

We saw the light and we came in, your Honour. Thank God, you are a good man... No, we're fine standing. We saw some light and... What, this? Our rings, your Honour. They're our hoops and rings. We're the body-piercers. We write on them, draw on them, play around on them as if on sand. Our bodies are what little we have left, your Honour. For us, piercing ourselves and covering our skin with unusual symbols, strange even to our eyes, is about making something that's beautiful. Where else can we still do that, except on our skin?... Absolutely. By piercing our bodies as if to make us remember something, your Honour, as if to remind us, we are definitely saying something that perhaps we're not capable of expressing—or perhaps are simply unwilling to express—logically, in words, or empirically, by our actions; nonetheless, whatever that thing is, we're saying it. What is it? It's this: we no longer have anywhere to live. And we're burning up. Born twenty or thirty years ago (give or take a few years, our exact age is neither here nor there) at this point, all we have left in this world is ourselves, unlike you, your Honour, you Sir, who have the museum of nostalgia (your memories) readily at hand as a bulwark against the insults of time, because you at least have lost something. We, though, have nothing. We are advancing naked, not a word, deed, speech, truth, sky, nor promise that we can trust anymore. Which is why we do what we do, with our studs, with our piercings. Yes. We're putting ourselves out there, making an exhibition of ourselves, true, but take a closer look and you'll see that the visible and hyper-visible symbols we're displaying, which run like water fleas off the greasy suint of our boredom, convey one desire only: a wish to disappear, to abandon the corpse of this dead country, your Honour, the corpse of the future which has been devoured by the generation of guzzlers who brought us into this world, after a final resounding burp punctuating a final majestic meal (they plundered the buffet). That's what we're talking about. We no longer want to share our breath with the breath of death. We want places where we are free to come and go, where we can love each other, listen to our own music, places where the air we have struggled to breathe for twenty years, your Honour, since the moment we opened our eyes to the carnage left by those who created us, places where that air no longer exists. We no longer have any beliefs. The family, the couple, the nation, engagement, militancy, manifestoes—Surrealist, Dadaist, Futurist—religion, transcendence, connection, none of it exists anymore.

That's not right.

We still have the climate.

We were forgetting the climate, your Honour.

But who seriously wants the climate to be their battle? Who wants to elevate the act of breathing to the status of a human right? Nobody asks to suffer, do they? And yet this is where we are. So, in the absence of nostalgia, we'll retreat into our own museum, your Honour, the museum of contradiction. A museum where, on the one hand, there's a desire to inflict a little pain on ourselves and, on the other, a desire to make ourselves feel good. Because we want both, we want to live and we want to die, to believe and to reject, to love each other and kill one another, caress each other both gently and violently. Which is why we go through some phases where our body, nourished by organic grains, is both our sole purpose and an end in itself, and others where we destroy ourselves draining the vodka-filled goatskin of despair. In the museum of contradictions, all is misery, but your Honour, we never relinquish the thought that sometimes a shitheap might just spawn a rose. And we smile. That's how we live. Besides, nothing around us is given its true name anymore. Compulsive lies are known as 'omissions'. Mere trifles pass for priorities. And that's how life is, your Honour. When words start meaning the opposite of what they say, your Honour, or the opposite of what they claim to be, everything just gets messed up, doesn't it, nothing makes sense anymore . . . Right. Well, our heads are messed up. And then on top of all that, we're apathetic.

We no longer know how to think, nor what we ought to be thinking, and then, if we're tempted by anything, it's to take up arms. So, in order to rouse ourselves, we pinch ourselves by burying studs and metal hoops in our flesh. Or we do it with tattoos. Or with rings and sometimes even chains. Our hair is silver and gold, and we wear T-shirts with slogans. One day we stuff ourselves with food, the next we fast. Sport-loving on Thursdays, alcoholics the rest of the week, which is how we delude ourselves that we're free. But the reality is, we're done in. Just like our elected representatives, who talk and talk and no longer sleep. Like everyone else, your Honour. Hollowed out. Done in. One day, though, we voted. It's a while ago now and already it's hard to believe it ever happened, your Honour. And yet we did. We did because people like you told us to. And you know what? Nothing. Nothing happened, and the women and men whose names we pulled out of the hats at the ballot boxes sank just as quickly back into oblivion. And all that has happened since is that we've fallen ill. We've lost our taste for things. We've lost our energy. And we've lost hope. So that's why we came in (we saw some light and we came in).

Look, the other day, we took ourselves off to the sea. We took the 10.01 train. There were quite a few of us. Quite a few, and we were utterly exhausted. Once we arrived at our destination, there were people everywhere, your Honour. But for us, used to battling our way through the millennial shitstorm, leaving the bedlam of a railway station is the work of a matter of seconds. Bat of an eyelid and we were out of there. Then we walked. And we saw it. To begin with, it was flat and still, and some of us no longer remembered ever having seen it, while others truly hadn't ever seen it. They laughed, your Honour. And we leaped into the water. Then, every one of us lay down on our towels, our energy drinks next to us. It must have been four in the afternoon. And then, your Honour, in the midst of our happiness, the sea started to rise. It happens sometimes. The sea can breathe, like money. And just like that, the beach started to melt away, like the streets of our towns, like the hope in our hearts, it melted away and by five o'clock, it had been reduced to a ridiculously small stretch of pack ice where we felt like penguins, your Honour, all crammed together, one on top of another. At the same time, there were people who had come, like us, to hear the sea breathe (although they came in cars, while we took the train), and they were sitting in VIP bars, looking at us, thinking everything was just fine, drinking away, laughing, listening to music. In the midst of all this we took the chance to have one last quick dip, then hurriedly dried ourselves and, while we had dusted off our misfortunes, your Honour, at the very moment when our misfortunes were starting to dissolve with the effect of the salt, some people started to go at each other like dogs. Only some, your Honour. Not everyone. We were not involved. As we said, we only wanted to look at the sea. We wanted to hear it breathe, and feel some inspiration from the sky and the horizon. But we were asked to leave. We were asked to pack up our stuff and get out of there and that's what we did, your Honour. The constabulary asked us to move on. They reclaimed the sand. Took it back from us. Did the same with the sea. Took it away from us. First, it was the air. And now, not only do we have to account for our actions, your Honour, but we'll no longer be able to go to the seaside, because the coast is banned for people like us. People with piercings and flaws. People of dubious means and sometimes no means at all. That's why we're here, why we came in. There was some light and we wanted to talk. To say this: soon, we too will fight. We don't know against whom, for the enemy's face is blurry and things no longer speak their name because that's the order of the day. But we will fight, and for that, we seek in advance your forgiveness. We will fight it out, one against another, your Honour. We'll kill each other, like dogs in a frenzied fury, because we'll be locked up in towns which will have been abandoned by every sand bank, by the air, by the water and by the wind. Forgive us, your Honour. Forgive us. We'll do filthy, ugly things to those whose paths we cross, whatever they do to us, and even if they do nothing to us, perhaps especially then. We will be evil for the sake of being evil. Just as we are punished for the sake of punishing. Moreover, we'll be so hungry that we'll kill for a French fry and the taste of some lemon mayonnaise, not to mention some prawn fritters . . . Set fire to the sand? Yes, we'll set fire to the beaches, as well as to the beach loungers you have to pay for and the black, dirty, polluted wave of money that washes over everything and gobbles up the lot. Your Honour, forgive us. And (let's see this through) we'll attack the weasel-words, too, of those who speak in our place knowing nothing about us and, having been set alight, one after the other, those words will be reinvented, their meaning and power restored.

We say this out of love, your Honour, based on the faith of our despair and our love. Yes, we'll fight like dogs, and we'll pierce ourselves, using ever sharper tools, for if our anger doesn't do it, we, we will explode.

2

Regarding a troop of pyjama-clad escapees

My darling, we did it! We escaped through the window, Uncle Tom, Marcel, Martha, André, Anna the Eldest, the Great Instructor (the former swimming teacher), and then there was us, the quarrymen from the valley. We did a runner. We did it! In those first few moments, as we set off, I felt for my heart to check it was still beating because I thought I might be dying. Then I smiled, because it was as if the cold were gouging a hole in my cheek. I could feel it rushing between the grey peaks of my dentures, caressing my tongue, speaking to me. It felt gentle. Did I say it was gentle? It felt good, and I could feel the cold of the gravel, too, in the car park where our walk began. The nursing home was shrouded in darkness, we had gone out through the dining hall window, and when I turned back to make sure we really were doing what we were doing, all I could see was the string of fairy lights around the Christmas tree at reception. That damned reception! Bloody nursing home! We'll never go back. Did I say that already? I think I did. We started walking. My throat was tight at the thought of leaving old Uncle Albin behind. He had the bed next to mine in the barracks. But Uncle Tom said he would hold us up with all his issues, the lungs, the heart, and the rest of it. I hung back a few moments, looking at the building where I had just spent the longest ten years of my life. The most expensive, too. Well, what do you do. Seeing the reflection of the Christmas lights sparkling in my eyes for just a little too long, Uncle Tom nudged me gently, he turned back, gave me a nudge he did, and said that old Uncle Albin would be better off tucked up in his own bed, nice and quiet, then he thwacked me, got me right where I feel my sciatica, and we were off. We'd made it through the car park and were now making our way slowly along the main route des Menhirs, not far from the Croix-Colette junction. Uncle Tom was bellowing. Barking orders. Martha Lawarrée reached out for my hand, she's the widow of Émile, the florist you always thought was so handsome. She was struggling to keep up. Struggling just as much as Anna; the Great Swimming Instructor thought he could carry her but the only place he was lifting anybody was in his own loopy mind. Did I say that old Uncle Albin wasn't with us? Martha was wearing pyjamas. She gave me her hand and I just kept talking to her, encouraging her along. We were all in pyjamas, Uncle Tom and the others, the quarrymen from the valley, all of us. A fine band of loonies we must have looked! Did I already say that? I can't remember any more. We were walking along the main road, each of us wearing slippers and pyjamas, because that was the official kit of the

Six Blueberries nursing home. Anyone would think they were having a go! The names they pick for these old people's homes, my love, they're ridiculous . . . Anyone would think they were out to poke fun. Well, let them, I say. The cold was now gouging a hole in my cheek. But I could feel it crawling up through the lower reaches of my body, too, just like it did in 1940. Feet, calves, the works. They gave nothing at the Six Blueberries to our kind. No shoes, no work, no beer worth the name. Did I say that I miss you, that I still love you? For ten years they spread plastic catch-alls around every one of my meals, put straws in the pink cordial they call wine, and shouted in my ear to get me to settle down. They said I was agitated, that I was hard of hearing, that I had lost my marbles and had that memory disease. Did I say that in all that time you were always there in my thoughts, Lucia? We used to get vanilla pudding to finish off our meals. You know I never could stand vanilla pudding. It's an insult to your tastebuds. Except that in there, our tastebuds counted for nothing; we were just a problem that had to be managed (Uncle Tom, well, he was an eighty-four-year-old problem, ninety-six for Anna, eighty-three for me, eighty-nine for the Great Swimming Instructor and the same for Martha Lawarrée, the widow of the florist you used to think was so handsome). And yet all the while, as the carers insisted we swallow down our little pots of vanilla pudding, I had you at my side. I was getting married to you every day of the week. Good Lord above, how many times didn't I ask for your hand in marriage while they washed me down, Lucia, like I was some wounded beast or a piece of meat! How many times didn't I laugh to think of you up there, leaning against your star, unable to understand why your husband was being treated like that, a man who had spent his life splitting rocks at the quarry! Three o'clock in the morning. It was almost three o'clock when Uncle Tom raised a hand because Martha was no longer keeping up. Martha had given up at the rocky shoulder, smack bang in the middle of the slope of La Redoute. Did I say that Martha couldn't keep going? Uncle Tom raised his hand and had this to say, 'She'll stay here. If we want to make it home, there's nothing else for it'. And he pulled off his pyjama top, placed it around poor Martha's shoulders, and pressed on, saying we were nothing but a bunch of laggards and that we would do well to hurry it along a little. We walked on in the cold, keeping to single file but no longer next to the main road. In the forest, through the spruce plantations which I hate and past the singing swallow-holes which I love, alongside felled trees on which, I swear, you could still clearly make out the shell marks from 1940. The bark black at the point of impact. Great patches as big as my hand, Lucia. Completely black. The sun had risen. We were walking towards Belle Roche, where I had fronted up my entire life. Did I say it has changed a lot since we were young, the Belle Roche site? The orchids have disappeared and it has been taken over by gravel, entire roads full of stones and holes. All of a sudden, Anna didn't want to go on anymore either. She came to a standstill on the path. Looked at us, one after the other. Didn't say a word. She bade us farewell. Then lay down beneath a section of barbed wire, picked herself up again, then headed off through the Moutards' field, the one below her house. A few minutes later, it was Marcel's turn. Then André's. Everybody took off in a different direction, each of them harbouring a plan for finding their way back, to the home they had lost. André, then, wanted to take a flower to lay on the grave of his wife, Nina, who had died the year before at the Mimosa nursing home. Did I say that Nina died the year before? I don't think you were that fond of her. By the time midday came around there were only a few of us left. The quarrymen, Uncle Tom and the Great Swimming Instructor. We couldn't take another step. Exhausted, my love. To the point where we hid behind an abandoned hut and ate the vanilla puddings we'd brought with us just in case. Uncle Tom was smiling. Then he turned out one of the custards, like he was pulling the pin from a grenade, and tossed it up onto the hut, yelling, 'Everybody down! On your bellies!' And before the pudding fell back to the ground, he made a sound like a grenade and everyone burst out laughing. My love (I can say 'love' now), I laughed like them, with them, but without further ado and, like the others before me, I said my goodbyes to Uncle Tom and headed off towards the lake. For months the carers have been telling me over and over, I've got a screw loose, saying I'm a few fries short of a bag. 'Fries short of a bag', 'Ans Elmer's disease'. Every day it's more of the same. But I didn't listen to them. I didn't listen because I haven't forgotten a thing. Quite the reverse. I live rooted in my memories of the asters and zinnias in the garden at home. Better yet, those memories are rooted in me. The images float to the surface, like the swell of the sea, and your fool of a husband is submerged in them. They're the ones calling it 'forgetfulness'. But if you ask me, my memories have never been so plentiful or so pure. No slag there. I headed towards the lake. Did I say that the quarry has become a lake? I couldn't believe my eyes. An artificial lake created by a dam. The whole village, Lucia. The whole village was swallowed up, the house, the garden, the asters and the roses you so used to love. I don't know how many years ago it was now. I was cold, night had just fallen, and it was no longer a hole in my mouth I could feel, no, the cold was shifting towards my heart. So I pulled off my pyjamas, like I did on our wedding night. And I lay down on the water. Then I kicked my legs vigorously, like I do with Madame Reuters—or is it Reulers?—the physio, and I imagined I was wearing a mask and snorkel. I took a big breath and I left it behind, everything around me, everything I could no longer bear to see. Dear love of my life. Did I say what a delicious feeling it was? The best. I started to sink, but I was no longer afraid, because my heart had grown used to the feeling. There was rubbish everywhere. I ignored it. I made myself an imaginary torch and turned it on, Lucia. Now I could feel the weight of the water on my chest. My lungs were empty but happily so. For a long time I kept diving, ever deeper, imagining you under the apple tree on your thirtieth birthday, reading those books of poetry you could never be without. The temperature was mild. Reeds brushed past me, billowing like the hair of the dead, and it was then, while I swam among it, surrounded by the hair of the dead, that I saw it, with my own eyes I saw the roof of the old Saint Nicolas church, my beauty, and what looked like the terrace of the Café Émilien where we used to play cards on a Sunday afternoon. Further on, the garden. And between two paths, there you were, hanging out the washing, and there was I, breaking up clods of earth before putting in some potato plants. Maurice Chevalier on the radio at Aunt Rosalie's. Then your hand like a salve on the nape of my neck and those words, 'I love you,' which follow me and carry me as I descend into the quarry with my hammer and chisel and the beginnings of the sciatica that will plague me for life. Every now and again, I raised my eyes towards the surface where I imagined a little rowboat was waiting, but there was no longer any surface and no longer any little boat. In fact, I was no longer even swimming. I had reached the ideal depth. For want of reaching the stars, I had sunk to the point where I could touch the blue curtains of the bedroom where so many times we had made love and where, with my elbows on the sill of the window through which I used to shoot at magpies and crows, I could see you smiling under the cherry tree, beckoning me to join you, your lips mouthing the letters of my name, one by one. Who was it who said that to grow old is to forget? I've rediscovered the memory of things. I've swum until I could picture myself once more as a child. Little Jean wearing his shorts out there in the fields. If only they knew, back at the Six Blueberries, how comfortable I am here. In the distance, my father is running towards me, shouting at me to watch over the cows and the flock instead of letting them scatter to the winds. I can smell Mama's scent, dizzyingly strong. In the orchard, you pick an apple for me, standing on the ladder, your buttocks round like two of Aunt Rosalie's walnut breads. You're singing a favourite aria, one of Verdi's, the sky is clear. Did I say, too, my hair is white? That there is no longer any trace of darkness within me? Forgetting is a second remembering, Lucia. The window through which everything returns. Did I already say all that? Dear heart, what would you say to a game of cards? Would you marry me?

3

Regarding the castle in ashes

We've come in so that we might have a word, Oh-Neighbour-of-Ours. A great many of us have come to speak with you, ma'am, my brother and I, along with our vast and undefeated forces. My brother won't be speaking. I'll be his voice. Can you see him properly, my brother? Do you have a good view of him? Look at him. He's over there. He can't hear a word I'm saying. He's staring at the bird of prey, a kite, that would like to carry off the chickens from Lulu's place, but as far as he's concerned, there's no kite and no more hens at Lulu's. My brother is damaged, the lights are on and nobody's home, Oh-Neighbour-of-Ours. And ma'am, it's your fault.

Can you see him?

His eyes and the way he's smoking that piece of vine, the lines that fracture and furrow his shattered child's face. I've been looking at them, the lines on my young brother's face, looking at them since yesterday, then I look at his hands, his short, stubby fingers and his nails filthy with chicken shit from Lulu's place. The long nails and the whittled down fingers of my very little brother, crouched on the embankment, his backside between two clumps of tansy. His fingers which, quick as a flash, tear open the Doritos packet that I bought from the Old Bag (that's what we call Berthe, the grocer), but which tremble too much for him to eat them. Even if people say I'm naughty and I cop my fair share of beatings and hidings at home because of my tempers and moods, it hurts to see him like that. It hurts. So I crumble the chips into his hand, and he eats them, Oh-Neighbour-of Ours, then he forgets.

It's noon.

Yesterday, he was still with me, he was still my brother. And now, he's vegetable matter. He blinks his eyes, lowers his cap, tries to pick himself up, looks for some shade, and there he goes, licking his fingers again, the kite still hovering above him. Its shadow immense. If only we could live in its shadow, the eternal shadow of the great kites. If only we could haul ourselves up just a little, us kids from the school of hard knocks. If only we could see beyond the mud and the everyday trench warfare. Every day we're in the bowels of the trenches. Our parents couldn't give a damn, because we belong to that category of kids who've had no pampering and who've been rudely dumped on this earth. No swimming pools, no lessons, no tenderness and no suggestion of any home tutoring for kids who are destined to be decision-makers. Not for us an employee's pink swipe card. We'll remain filthy, dishevelled and lice-ridden. For as long as there is the sky, Oh-Neighbour-of-Ours, the towering vast sky into which we dive every day.

We have our bikes.

They're our wings.

Our means of escape.

Without them, it would be the death of the Delwaere kids. Charly and Jules Delwaere. The cursed children of Marie-Christine Castagne and Jean-Philippe Delwaere, also known as Phiphi, or the Boxer.

Home, for us, is down there, a long way from the properties sprouting verandas, extensions and solar panels, owned by the likes of you. We, on the other hand, have a shack with a garden shed. You know the one. You didn't really feel like coming all the way down to our place yesterday. And yet you did. You parked some distance away. You walked down the path and you didn't like the sound of the gravel, because it was as if it were soiling you, sullying both your soul and your flesh (a small stone sitting like a weight on your heart, Oh-Neighbour-of-Ours). You rang the doorbell. Our mother opened for you. And then, you told her what you had seen. What you had just seen. Seen us doing. Then you left and, ever since, my brother has had the face he has. Take a long, hard look at him. He's watching the kite, looking at the sun. I'm stuffing chips into his mouth but I'm not even sure the Boxer spared him his sense of taste. As a result of your words, Oh-Neighbour-of-Ours. You're the one with the words, the words to wound. That's how you hurt people, you lot with your green landscaping, always on the move, swift, well-groomed and appealing, you people who are active, slender, sweet and forgiving, with your clay face masks and generally exquisite fruit teas. That's how you wound.

You opened your great gob.

A night went by.

And in the meantime, the tornado struck. Papa. Phiphi. There was Jules, on the ground, his jaw dislocated, the bone split down the middle of his chin. Mama screaming and smoking, terrified, unable to move. It was your fault. You did that. But there's something else we're going to say: we knew we weren't allowed to go play in the abandoned chateau, we had known that since it had burned down. But we went anyway. We did. Not just to get away from the Boxer, but because someone's there, in the castle, a presence.

An old man who looks like Uncle Benjamin. Phiphi's brother. We loved him. He dropped dead in the middle of the farm at the age of 44. Thwack! Three years ago. And since then, life has been a desert. The world withered with his death. We would look at the geese on his pond, we would look at his marshland, we'd wander around his cabin, but he was no longer anywhere to be seen. He'd drawn the curtain.

Then, one day, the chateau burned down. It went up in flames and it was as if those flames had shown him the way. And he came back! Yes! Now we could see him stretched out in the ashes. We heard him cough. We spoke to him. You cough a lot. True, he'd say. Will it pass? Yes. You sure? Yes. Why? Everything passes, he would say.

On other occasions, he would make a fire for us, then he would take us away from the ashes for a walk, in the fresh air, to places neither Mama nor the Boxer would find. This is the shortest path, he would say. The fastest way to get to the spring. We'll have a drink there! Come on! With him, life seemed beautiful. And so it was, Oh-Neighbour-of-Ours. Now my brother wears a . . . Yes, it's a prosthesis. You know the correct words. You're sorry. You're innocent. Of course you are. Because, like all those who are guilty these days, no, you didn't want there to be any dramas.

Uncle Benjamin.

When we got to the chateau in ashes and couldn't find him, we went looking for him. And if, unable to admit defeat, and despite our best efforts, he still wouldn't show himself, we would stay there, sitting on the stone, waiting for him as we looked at the sky with the kite hovering above the charred beams. We no longer felt like eating chips, we no longer felt like anything. Sometimes, he would tell us things we didn't understand. The fact that fathers do what they can and that, when you're too close to the ones you love, you can end up hurting them. Things like that. Then we would see him bring out his Opinel knife, pick up a branch from an elder tree and carve a sweet little flute, a thin pipe. For us. He would teach us about the birds. Is it a chaffinch, Uncle? Wrong! A nesting lark! What about over there, Uncle? A honey buzzard, it has markings on its flight feathers, stripes beneath its wings. And over there? An aeroplane, you imbeciles, that's a Lufthansa plane!

Let us just say this.

We knew well enough that yesterday was the last time we would go to the chateau. The day before, Phiphi had made it clear he would kill anybody he found hanging around there. We had been warned. So much so that we did our best to conceal ourselves as we made our way there. We climbed the ladder. We picked our way across the beams, balancing, falling, then picking ourselves up again . . . What were we after? To say our goodbyes, to have no regrets. So when we saw him, we knelt down in front of him. There was something God-like about him, stretched out in the filth at the back of the armoury room. Immaculate. Unchanging. We said nothing. Then, 'A skeleton buried in muck,' said my brother. 'A mighty fine skeleton.' And he started to touch it, talking to it as if to say 'Farewell'. Then, turning back to me, he said, 'That's that, then, let's go, we're out of here.' But for whatever reason, I decided to lie down next to him, next to Uncle Benjamin, alongside my dreams and wishes. I grabbed his pipe—yes, even dead he was smoking—I pulled it from his fingers and slipped it between my lips. That's right, I shoved Uncle's pipe between my lips and, imitating his very deep voice, I said that all this was our secret, that nobody would know what had happened here, in the chateau. The three of us. Our games. The joy. Then I kissed his cheeks, his forehead and his chest. And in my child's voice this time, making an enormous effort not to dissolve into tears, I said, 'Alright? It'll be our secret.' Then I stood up, pocketed his pipe and stood there, with my brother, my little brother, receding into the night, watching Uncle's body grow ever more distant, like when you fly over a landscape, a landscape you're leaving behind, farewelling. Then, we went home and there you were, Oh-Neighbour-of Ours. 'I saw them playing in the chateau.' Those words, pointing at Jules. Good God above, why him?

4

Regarding paradise

We, too, saw the light, and entered. Merciful Lord, in your goodness... Alright. We won't invoke you. You don't like it when people invoke you. We came in because it was quiet. More because of that than because of the light, yes, it was the quiet we liked. The same as when we used to water the basil plants on our antiquated verandas or, when motionless in the bath, we felt like we might dissolve, Lord our God. Forgive us. We won't invoke you anymore.
... Who are we? The women who always felt we needed to make ourselves invisible, who were never able to remain on the surface of things, and who turned our backs on life, for fear of falling.

We are not at peace.

We never have been.

And, knowing that we are easily startled—frightened of everything—and that we have been brought up under the bell jar of religion and universal lies, we have never found our place. Ever.

We are incensed by the slightest thing.

A car that narrowly misses us? The noise of a motorbike? A pigeon dropping? The simple beating of wings? And we jump! Fear? Our whole lives we have felt it. When we were little, we felt it in the bus that would take us to boarding school. And then when we used to answer the unholy questions of the good Sisters in that very boarding school. We used to feel it when, later on, boys started to ogle our asses and also, at that same time in our lives, at every step which took us away from our beloved homes in the middle of nowhere, in those crazy towns where we feared being mown down by some automobile, or some laundry van, à la Roland Barthes.

Fear of abandonment.

Fear of our fathers and the bleak lineage to which we belonged: priests who didn't have the strength to become priests—their flesh was on fire—curt, violent sorts who would have been better off, it seems, becoming monks, reflecting your glory. But so be it. There was something else: we felt abstract. Has anybody ever said anything like that to you? Empty and unsullied, even when we were meant to be at the top of our game. That's what we were. Who we are.

Have we ever been at the top of our game? No, because we've suffered from it our whole life. The fear, that is. Scared witless. The only place where we could justify our existence was in the one metre sixty-by-two metres of our bed. To sleep that we might die and not have to hear the rattlesnake clatter of madness, which nonetheless bellowed within us drowning out our fathers' pious cries and follies. Our family? A family of sleepers, corpses who have not yet had the last word. So, on the one hand our bed. And, on the other, our work at the university: digging through the archives of the museum of human thought. Thirty years straight, searching and rummaging through archives belonging to a time when people like Barthes (of course, we were interested in a much earlier period) considered it worthwhile to devote their lives to thinking, and then, through their writing, to clarifying what they had seen. Their thoughts, like so much else that is invisible, rendered visible, if you like, by their words. It hardly matters. It doesn't happen anymore, for such is the way of things: they end up being devoured, nothing remains of them. But we're getting sidetracked. We came in for the sense of calm inspired by your 'office'. A place where what we have to say could be heard and where we could ask questions, perhaps, while awaiting your verdict.

Be gentle, won't you?

Look, yesterday, we met a man. Who, when he approached us, with the miserable taint of hunger in his eyes, immediately provoked in us a feeling of disgust. We wouldn't normally use that word. We're using it now, though, because right from the outset he made us feel nauseous. About thirty. But poverty is precocious so who knows? Maybe he was only twenty. Korean. Mad. Terrible . . . What? Not at all! Nobody's less racist than we are!

Chad? We love that country.

We think it all belongs to everyone, the world, the sea and the endless stars in the sky. Just last year we were in Bali!

What's more, if it just so happens that we're unable to give anything, we're happy to say we're not stingy. We're left-leaning. Resolutely so. We don't want any poverty or unhappiness. Even if the facts suggest otherwise. What do you do? There's what you want and what you get.

We are mothers, yes. To begin with, we used to think we were perfect mothers, but we rapidly realised, for example, that we weren't so keen on listening to our children. Jacques. Paul. Robert. Elisabeth. Lison. Coming home from school, the unbearable stench of the canteen still clinging to them, they would talk to us (childhood as one interminable monologue intolerable to the adult ear), 'We did this, Mother, then this, and then that.' And how did we react? You want us to tell you? All these things, told through the snot of their blocked nostrils, all of it went straight over our heads. Do we love them any the less for it? No.

In any event, as a result of our work at the museum of lost thoughts, we got to the point where we no longer heard them. For either we would be thinking about those ancient areas of knowledge or about our sleep. So that once they turned nine (up until then we would still listen with half an ear, seeing as they might still have needed us) we stopped living in the same world altogether. From that point onwards, we were merely going through the motions, mindlessly and repetitively: driving them to sport, making Bolognese sauce, setting the table properly with suitable plates, wishing them bon appétit. Were we dreadful mothers? Were we worse than any others? We know they loved us. Somehow in the midst of it all, that is enough for us. In any event, we couldn't have behaved any differently. We all make stupid mistakes and we all have our hands tied, even mothers with a job, an education, and husbands who are as rich as they are absent. Even for us, you know, life is hard. Doesn't matter. We're here now, at your right hand. And it's not the slightest bit important whether life is a struggle or not. Isn't that right?

So then, yesterday. We were walking through the centre of town. We found ourselves outside the sushi place, or the spectacles place, or the red lentil place where we'd just stocked up (it was about five in the evening) when, while we were rooted to the spot, trying to remove a tiny pebble from one of our heels, one foot in the air and leg half bent, chipped toenails exposed to the gusty wind, we saw him. His vacant eyes. He was staring at us and heading towards us with his miserable begging cup and . . . Too late. The guy stopped a few metres away, he needed three euros for a bed at the hostel. They all want a bed at the hostel. Let's just say this: he was wearing neither a mask nor any other facial covering, so we felt not only exposed, but also in danger. We're all mindful of contamination. The fact remains he was no more than a few centimetres away when, seeing his mouth like a water flea targeting our integrity, we put our shoe back on, without removing the pebble, and made our escape.

There you have it.

Twenty minutes go past.

We've forgotten about the shyster and are swooning at the window of the pancetta bar, one of the best, in the same neighbourhood as all the poodle bars. And suddenly—

wham!—there he is again. 'Monsieur,' we say, at the same time as we turn away, 'we don't have anything!' And with the same gesture we'd use to shoo away a horse fly, or a wasp on a rum baba, we ask him to leave us alone. And there he is, stabbing his finger at us (at us, smartly dressed and proud in our old age thanks to the prostheses of wealth), stabbing his finger at us, as if to say, 'That's not true, you're lying.' He leaves, with the tender, slow gait of a person lugging not only his corpse but his own tomb. A resignation we found pleasing. And which then had us feeling rather stunned. Yes, just for a moment, children of the catechism and rosary that we are, daughters of Jesus, we had just been thinking we were happy, that it was a good thing this unfortunate Korean—or was he Chinese?—was no longer standing between one of our many pleasures and another of our many pleasures, or between one of our many delights and another of our many delights.

The clock had just struck six in the evening. The pancetta was giving us the eye and, refusing to let ourselves be diverted by depression and, most of all, not wanting to miss our chance, we bought no less than 230 grams.

Absolutely, 230 grams.

Lord, enough to make us split our knickers!

But no.

Because, once we were back home, it seemed as if the little pebble we had not removed from our shoe, as if that damned pebble was now weighing on our heart. It weighed heavier and heavier, Lord, like a little stone weight, the weight of fear and regret. And in the time it takes to say, 'Oh dear,' there was nobody left to say 'Oh dear'. Here we were, at your side. So then, paradise?

5

Regarding that place beyond the Wall

Good morning. Our names are Sarah, Jessica, Steph, Louisette and Manon. And we regret having brought our children into the world. Let it be said. We're very sorry about it all. Forgive us. It's not the worst thing to have done, but we ought not to have done it. We wanted a clear horizon, where the very essence of their beings would be content, where nothing would collapse. A habitable world.

Now, even if it is impossible to describe in so many words, if the monster bringing us to our knees has too many faces to be identified, and if, when we shoot, it is not fury we are lacking but simply a target, we will scream it out nonetheless: we can no longer bear the 'system' and we no longer believe in it, quite independently of the fact that in so many ways it is beyond us, and that we will never get to the heart of it. On the other hand, there are our nerves. We know the world is falling apart. And we know it because our nerves, too, are going to pieces. More wildfires, more boats sinking, more warming, more tsunamis. Its sickness is manifesting in us, only on a smaller scale. Our anxieties, our sleeplessness are those of the world, its pains, its contradictions. The world is hurting through us, it is suffering, and it is making it known.

Sure, we might have had our measure of joy, but times are what they are and the pain is hitting us. It's hitting hard. One day, we're surprised that the trees are causing us pain, the birds. The next, in days to come, it will be our children's games that hurt. We're looking for a way to heal ourselves. Or to hope? Something to hold on to? We're trying to find a name for the centuries still to come. A name that is possible.

When we were little, we already held a grudge against the 'system'. We've never believed in it. Anarchists, through and through. So, when our fathers' alarm clocks came spluttering to life so they could go off to sell sports cars, or pour concrete into car parks in front of the shopping centres they were building, we were dreaming of Kiko and James (that's what we called our cats), dreaming of their warmth; we loathed school which was making us soft and compliant, we wanted the tenderness of our mothers, that was all, just the tenderness of those marvellous women who had always done what they could, as much with us as with the males in their lives. Thatcher was on the radio, 'There is no alternative.' But our fathers continued to kill themselves at the coalface, and their homes, our homes, were improved over the months and years, this one having the garage tiled, that one getting a granny flat, this one a real garden path and right at the end of it, a terrace and built-in barbecue.

And yet we would play over the top of all that, over the

top of the wildfires and the violence of a world where the tiniest parcel of air was at risk of being sold off. We won't re-play the match, but now they're here, our kids, what do we do? How do we hide them from car parks served up with a side of concrete? How do we protect them from the diggers? We've thought about it. And that's how we came up with the idea that we could just take off. Which is precisely what we did. Three years ago. We left our old jobs. Primary school teachers. Librarians. Systems managers. Nurses. Judges. See you later! We were young, we were beautiful. Our bosses loved us. Because, if you don't mind us saying so, we had put our dreams on the back burner in order to serve their interests and a whole range of causes having nothing to do with us (this story ought to be rewritten as a millefeuille of causes bearing no relation to us, but which we internalised to such an extent they became indispensable, legitimate). In short, we were the instruments of a dull driving force that was constantly bawling at us: Work! It was the sixth of June 2018, we remember it well. We shook hands with our bosses, handed in the keys to our apartment, closed the gate to the city and took the other path, cutting across the fields. A different path, one that was just for us, even if there were many of us doing it, and it was just another form of herd mentality. We don't give a damn. We don't regret it. Our days are more peaceful, our children close by. We have our chickens, we have the seasons. We refuse to consume chemicals and no longer produce any waste. Because either we eat it, or we make it disappear in the steam of our compost... Our beauty masks? We use clay from the rock faces and droppings from our girls (our chickens). We no longer produce anything, we've eliminated everything down to our own breath.

Our breath is white.

Our exertions, white.

Our blood, flushed clean of any trace of animal product, white.

Clean minds for the beauty of the world, that's us.

Also, the more of us there are to do a job, the better it is. And the longer it takes, the happier we are! Seeing as the only gods we still believe in are those watching over the kitchen garden, we have our blueberries. They taste good, but better still, they have a soul. That's why we talk to them, touch them. Next to the yurt, an altar to our elders, to the trees, without whom we wouldn't be here, to the stars, who are our mothers and grandmothers, and to Pachamama. Every morning we cry, 'Glory be to the hair which once again has taken over our bodies, for it has given us new life!'

. . . Our children? Hans. Anouar. Jim. Juliette. Lucette. Marceline and Martin. They do odd jobs, they weave and knit Peruvian beanies in the barn where we cultivate our insects, which we eat, given that we no longer buy anything in the shops of death. Where can you find us? Head towards the woods. Somewhere there is a Green Wall, similar to the one Zamyatin talks about, a hidden wall, beyond which we have implemented our dreams, our own dreams as opposed to those of our fathers, but it's true they had none, and whatever they did, they did robot-like. We, on the other hand, want to see the return of the fireflies, of spring. To stay mischievous, light-hearted. We want our children to be clothed or not, to learn to read or not. We no longer want to play the role of super parents, who know everything, anticipate everything. We want to be authentic and are prepared to say that our children know more about life than we do. They wear the trousers. They represent the law, they are the law. Here, at our place, they're in charge of all that.

There's more: we believe that the gods are to be found hidden in the babble of our little ones. We believe the murmurings of the gods are to be found in them. What we teach them (and we say this with tears in our eyes, because we have never wavered on this point), is to listen with their heart, their emotions, and to accept everybody as they are. We talk to them: about positive things, in a positive fashion, so they can react positively.

No more orders.

No more preaching.

'You don't want to? Fine. You know what's best for you.'

That's how we do things. Then we weep in our sweat tent, our cheeks streaming, and sleep for three days straight beneath our green umbrellas, with our cat, Djidji, on our chest. It's a spiritual education, creative. A Shintoist approach . . . Our computers? Burned. Sure, it may have been possible to donate them, but we have our violent tendencies and it made us happy to burn them. Our list of contacts, our usernames, everything which makes up our apocryphal, sterile life? Burned, too!

The years have passed, but we have maintained the rage. Sure, we receive financial assistance from the State in the form of unemployment benefits, but that's a subject we'd rather not talk about (we all have our secret garden, don't we?). Also, whenever we have a little mishap, our mothers race to our rescue, rip out the bindweeds of despair and clean out the henhouse. Unlike our fathers, who are ashamed of us. Our mothers slip us a few pennies. Pennies which allow us to pay for things which our thirst for freedom has proven inadequate to provide us for free: the renting of asthma spacers, the 30 euros-a-month phone subscription fees (one telephone for all of us, it really doesn't cost anything), the blend of oil and petrol we use for our war machines, the vet for the animals and all of Batman's costs, Batman being our draft horse.

Sometimes our mothers sit down and make a fire, put a grill over the coals and cook fennel sausages like they used to. After which they launch into songs from the old days. And lay our pain to rest with marshmallows pulled straight from the hat of their tenderness. And it takes only a few moments for that feeling of abundance we so miss to return. The pure, well-rounded joy of our untainted childhood. The wild joy of our early years. The joy that means tomorrow we will get up and do it all again, digging our way ever further from the cursed places from which we have fled. And that, notwithstanding the fact we are worn down, exhausted, we will do just as those marvellous women did: improvise songs as a bulwark to our fear, in the very midst of it.

6

Regarding the cement mixers

We were born exactly forty years ago. Right next to the donkeys, in the miserable barn on the farm. Our mothers didn't have time to get to the local hospital in Bruyères. Which meant our fathers always thought of us that way: as donkeys. Donkeys and fools.

They had their obsessions, our fathers, putting fifty or so chickens in the three empty bedrooms of the farm and then regularly fronting up with a lamp in the middle of the night, hauling us from our sleep and forcing us to go and sit in the pool of light and stroke them, stroke his beloved chooks who'd be scoffing the seed tossed onto the lino. Other than that, we were quite normal children. We used to love mucking around in the mud and playing rough and tumble. We weren't so keen on our teachers. But yes, school was a breath of fresh air. The best part was when we used to take refuge in complicated calculations. That's where we'd find some peace. Our handwriting, though, that left a bit to be desired. Chicken scratchings, that's what our teachers used to say, whose eyesight we'd wrecked. By the age of ten, we knew how to drive our fathers' John Deere 3350s and could handle the big jobs on the farm all on our own. We knew how to milk the cows, we'd take the cattle to graze in the field behind the football pitch, we knew how to make them obey and knew how to shape the hay bales once summer arrived. One day, with our third hand, the one created by the very sharp pitchfork of our fathers, we even subdued the bull we used to call Hanscrouf. He'd been charging towards us! About our mothers, though, let's just say they've always been our fathers' personal assistants, in the sense that whatever they didn't do, our mothers did. Our dads were the cool guys on the tractors; our mothers, they dealt with the manure pits. They worked themselves to the bone. But nothing stopped them, and we never heard them complain about anything whatsoever, except some lower back pain. Our fathers tended to be layabouts at home. Once their working day was over, they'd sink into the sofa that was wedged about one metre thirty away from the television console, and nobody was allowed to say another word. Spent. They were done in from their day's work. They sat and drank and scoffed vast quantities of everything while they watched the news. After which the wooden staircase would creak under their weight when they disappeared upstairs with our mothers. They would close the door to their 'sanctuary', from which would burst forth all manner of eructations and yelping and which, despite our youth, we excelled in interpreting. Their bed would thump against the wall, the floor shook like it had hiccups and our mothers, whom we imagined to be dangling from the curtains, would scream atrocities while they, our fathers, with the exception of some crowing, remained spectacularly silent. On and on it went. Our childhood nights were filled entirely with the sounds of their thrusting heard through the floorboards. When they had finished, we'd have to follow them into the three rooms illuminated by the cold spotlights of their obsession. Feeding the chickens was a sport that, without us, didn't hold quite the same appeal.

'Come on! Get going!' And we would abandon our dreams, go upstairs and find ourselves in those three rooms littered with cackling droppings, watching them down cans of beer as they ordered us to stay sitting next to them. Right next to them. Sometimes, we thought we could hear them crying, but we chased such dark thoughts from our minds, for the idea that our fathers could weep, no, it was absurd.

When we ended up falling asleep, they would toss old flea-ridden blankets over us, and for us, never having felt loved by these men, that was heaven. They needed our strength, our youth. And had we not had those qualities, there's no doubt they would have sent us off quick smart to some boarding school for idiots beyond the Saint-Rémy fens. But when they did that, yes, when they kept us warm with those flea-ridden covers, it was heaven.

That said, school ended up becoming rather unpleasant. We slept a lot, slumped on our chairs. To the point where our teachers started to think we had tipped into that age when complicated maths sums stopped mattering, which was anything but true. At twelve, we loved nothing more than doing complicated sums. But we were so exhausted, and it was only getting worse, we weren't up for much. What's more, in the endless hours of class, we used to dream of a boy who was about our age, who could have been us, and who, in some ways, was us, but altered, changed, enhanced, because we didn't want a boy in our dreams who was just like us. We wanted a boy who was charming, calm, and who, let's just say, was not doomed the way we were. A boy with rich parents. Who loved him. That's right. A boy who would burst out laughing when the other children did and who loved fitting in with them, right up to the day when he felt 'strange', because he was attracted to other boys. To maths and to boys.

How often didn't we dream about him? Didn't we hope to be replaced by him? Reborn in him? How many nights, glued to our fathers' side, did we not wish to tell them about our obsession with that imaginary boy, imaginary, yet real, nonetheless? That's how it was.

When we were nineteen, European agricultural regulations forced farmers to reinvent themselves. Either they became engineers and managers. Or they snuffed it. History was headed in one direction, becoming inflated, ever larger (vast farms with thousands of animals cooped up as if in a zoo). Either the farmers followed suit, or they could walk out and leave the key under the door. As a result of which, we had to dedicate ourselves entirely to farming duties, instead of continuing to attend the business school where we had just started to hang out with people like you, dear neighbours. That was seventeen years ago, and from that point onwards, never again did we hear the sound of mattress springs squealing in the bedroom, nor hear the wall shifting. Europe, with its mad desire for growth, had wrung the boisterous joy out of our parents. These days? They're dead and the farm has been sold. As for us, we run a gardening business. We've started a family, whom we love. We have a shed filled to the brim with tools that trim, and cans of petrol for our machines. We get up early and we're remunerated for it, we have money. We work on the weekends too, for cash. And the richer the people who require our services, the more impressive the size of their swimming pool, the more we hit them up. We have Jeeps, too, they mimic the sound of our fathers' John Deeres very nicely. We have a pool. Nothing to complain about, no. In the morning, we lace up our steel-capped shoes at the window where the same blackbird sings the same sad tune, on the same tree. A milky coffee with three sugars and some bread with syrup and a slice of Gouda. People like us, we need our strength. And ears that can be seen from planet Neptune, because nothing makes us happier than clean, neat things, like a haircut that nicely reveals your ears, dear neighbours.

We have music playing in the background on our jobs. Bullshit radio stations, because they help us not to think. What's our thing? Noise. Keeping the motors of our machines running non-stop. It's annoying for you guys, of course. City-slickers who've come looking for some peace and quiet. As far as you're concerned, we're just rednecks. We still have some chickens, yes, because our kids are keen on them. But we don't have any patience with them, especially now they've picked up that weird sickness: they're sitting on unfertilised eggs, the damned things. Stopped eating. Stopped drinking. Don't sleep anymore! All because of some dream to be mums. Because this is how they think the 'Chicken' species is going to be perpetuated! Yesterday we made them get up. It was either that, or we were going to turn them into stock. Forty, yes. We're at the crossroads of life, don't want to waste any more time. Still, we're not about to change, despite your questions hinting in that direction. When the weather's good, we'll bring out the quadbikes and clean off the wheels on the plants and flowers on the embankments. Time passes, but it hasn't made us grow up. We're the reincarnation of our fathers, replicating their behaviour. Mowing. Trimming hedges. Beating the animals. Who said country folk love nature? Nature's a bitch for those who stop by. 'Nature? Something that takes up time and takes over everything else.' That's what our fathers used to say.

We think we're moving towards a life which resembles us or which will, one day, resemble us, but all we're doing is moving further away, because nothing resembles us. We're nothing.

. . . Do we still think about maths? Yes. And the little boy in our dreams, who liked boys? Of course. But we're happy working. So, yesterday we made some concrete. And you complained, because it was a Sunday. 'Why do you need to make concrete on a Sunday?' you asked. And we didn't know what to reply.

We do now, though. We've had a chance to think about it. We got the cement-mixer going because something strange happens against the backdrop of the noise of the motor. It makes the world melt away. Everything else falls quiet. Noise is a silence like any other, dear neighbours. When our dog barks, you hear noise; we hear silence. The close connection between noise and silence. Do we have faith in the material world? We want to cover it up. Do we have faith in the noise? We're just listening out for the voice of our fathers when they would toss those flea-ridden covers over us in that big, hen-filled room. That's who we are: people who want to make the world melt away beneath the howl of the cement-mixers, so that the trees, the sky, the cars, the pedestrians, and the incessant noise coming from mouths constantly filled with pointless words, all of it, ceases and no longer exists, or at least exists in some gentler form. The same form that you, too, hold dear.

We're made for each other.

Your yoga and the sound of our quadbikes, it's all one and the same. That's what we're saying. What our fathers were looking for. Europe destroyed them. At night (and we know this because their dreams are now ours), they used to lie listening to the flies and wasps take off from the walls of the garden path, panic-stricken by dreams of their own bodies being impaled. Our fathers would be in raptures, dreaming about the slightest little protrusion, the smallest ledge jutting out from the masonry, the sheer drop from the gates, the cellar windows, craving the teeth of the ploughs and rusted harrows lying around in the paddocks. Their hearts would start racing at the sight of them. Our fathers, they wanted to dissolve. Evaporate. Make no noise, do no harm. Broken men, destroyed by their labours, wanting only one thing: for there to be silence at their very core.

How about we have drinks tomorrow? What do you say, neighbours?

7

Regarding a diminished country

We have come consumed by remorse, Gran. Can't even manage a drink anymore . . . Our day? We were supposed to make something of it, like every other day, but we never got around to it. The day dawdles. Drifts. Drags on. Even talking irks us. But not as much as being silent. And not a day passes that we don't think of how lucky you were not to witness it all, this idiocy, which is supposed to be the key to what, Gran, you've got to ask yourself.

Our decline, that's all we have left.

The future lies in regret.

Loving one another, moving, weeping, being free, all of it has gone to hell since they shut down the world, and then threw away the key. Even more so for our dear President, nailed to the highest branches of that dead tree he persists in calling 'power', who maintains that everything, without fail, is for the best in the best of all possible worlds. 'What's the problem?' he says.

Yesterday, we felt so out of it that we spent the morning exercising, in shorts, in our miserable apartment on the rue des Cris-Continus. We smashed out the kilometres on our exercise bike, climbed endless hills. Didn't feel like going out. Not ready. Things drift. Drag on. Just needed to sweat, Gran. Eat some protein bars, pump up the muscles. Be alone. But because you do have to show your face a bit all the same, we changed into some clothes around midday and put on our face masks properly like we're supposed to, and out we went. We bought some vials of e-liquid at the e-cigarette tobacconist and drank a beer as we sat looking at the barges. It was mild. You could hear the wind talking. It was talking, Gran. And it was good. We felt good.

And, feeling more confident, we cleared our throat a little. A slight cough. Nothing serious. But no sooner had we done that, when some cop from the face-mask police jumped on us out of nowhere and hit us with a fine. Because we'd coughed, and the law says you can't, even though we were wearing our masks.

Fifty euros!

We didn't have it, of course. And we told him so. But he, not wearing any mask mind you, just said, 'Pay up!' And then we said, 'We don't have it. We don't have that amount.' So then he laid his paw on us, grabbed us by our hoodie and, as if we were out in the sticks somewhere in China or some other democracy-in-waiting, he repeated, 'Pay up', louder this time, dragging us along like worms and pointing to the sign banning coughing.

We signed the bank transfer, Gran. Then the sense of

things dragging on, the discouragement returned.

Without realising what we were doing, we started going up and down rue des Violettes, past the shuttered cinemas and the kitten cafés, whose walls we covered with the miserable blood from our enraged fists. That was yesterday. And every other day. Because that's our oxygen at the moment. Indoors, you suffocate. Outside, you still suffocate. Which just means you're reduced to changing up the form of torture or, if you'd rather, your poison.

The raw, absolute art of the dying. Who, knowing that everything is fucked, still can't help but hope.

When it came to hoping for a better world, you had your Mass. Father Reginster. His ears full of hair. We, too, have our museums of joy, our own personal paradise. A choice of two. The museum of regret, or the museum of nothingness, a big museum where you can self-virtualise. Two options. Either you can dream about the time when having a drink with friends was possible and fun; or you can post photos of your increasingly depilated bodies, with endless comments and incessant rants . . . What don't we agree with anymore? It's enough not to agree, Gran. Everything's connected. Which is good. What's true, what's false. What's honest, what isn't. A book, an ad. Promises, betrayals. You end up no longer knowing who to have a go at. But you have a go at them all the same.

Consumed by the stupor of having been reduced to this (so little intensity, so little joy), we're looking for the directions to life. Its location? What path should we take? Which horizons? Where are they, huh? Behind what hairy ears will we find the goddamned directions to life, Gran?

You know, yesterday, we took some photos of our new tattoo. On our butt cheek . . . the dragon, yes. And we posted them, because we were proud of them, even though, at the same time, we were already sick of them.

It takes nothing to make us happy.

It takes nothing to bring us undone.

Where are the beans to top and tail? What are our jobs for the day? Orders. We want your gentle-natured orders, your barking at us, Gran. You remember when we used to come and sleep at your place, in Fraiture, the village at the top of the hill with the same name, at number 54 on the street with the same name? When we would do some weeding, pick currants, wash the leeks and cut them up for the soups that were to be made, that's the direction we want to be headed. Now we've got our arses straddling the winged-back chair of nostalgia on the one hand and nothing on the other. Melancholic blackbirds. Miserable blackbirds that, regardless of whatever else they might do, never stop signalling to yesterday's child. Our whole life looks like that, like a child's room. Even our tattoos are the drawings of a child. What sort of a serious adult would draw a dolphin on their arm, Gran? Or a dragon, huh? Who would allow their triceps to be destroyed with the sketchy lines of an octopus drawn by their three-year-old son? What shops are we opening? Ali Baba caves of regret. What do they sell? Ashes from the years of our happiness. Radio cassette decks, Adidas tracksuits. Anything kitsch. Porcelain teacups, the same as yours, yes. The Villeroy & Boch.

Yesterday, we felt demoralised by such thoughts. The world was no longer enough for us. It was as if it were separating itself from us, like those sailing boats heading out of the harbour when you used to take us to Ostend and Middelkerke, once summer had arrived. It was as if nothing was staying with us for more than a few moments. As if our memory were a ghost that had been put through a juicer.

We felt a little bit on edge, yesterday.

That's why we walked all the way to the Basilica of Saint-Barthélemy and tiptoed our way through it.

We knelt down. We looked around us. The silence. The vaulted ceiling. The angels picnicking in the light.

Did we pray? No. But the silence, even though it was invisible, felt like some mythical creature, circling in the nave, behind the altar, everywhere. We remained like that, praying and thinking. Then, afraid that something would happen in our absence, or that we would miss something, we messaged our friends. Just to be sure. And you know what? Even though we glanced at our screens at perilously short intervals, something settled, grew calm, and we started to breathe more peacefully because, see, nothing had happened in our absence. Nothing of any significance. Nothing that was any more important than what was happening right there, in that bloody Basilica. Absolutely nothing at all, Gran.

Later, while taking a piss against the wall of the garden with the fake oranges which gives on to the forecourt, we noticed a series of posters relating to the lives of the saints. Little sheets, with simple words talking about those people you used to be so keen on, you and Gramps. Beautiful pictures, along with captions which spoke to us, drew us in. So that, for a moment there, we found ourselves passing from one saint's life to the next, unable to read anything carefully but, still, curious about everything. We read on, more and more absorbed. We couldn't get enough, and it was like leaving the world behind.

First up, Saint Jerome, in that little studiolo where he spent thirty years producing the Vulgate.

Saint Teresa Benedicta of the Cross, who spoke to us of the need, every morning, to gather together rather than to scatter apart.

Saint Anthony, of course, the saint of lost causes and objects, your favourite, Gran. Your idol. In a dead heat with Helmut Lotti.

And that's how an image of Gramp's face came back to us, he too in his own way having made his vows of simplicity. We saw his eyes again. And, along with them, we smelled the heady perfume of flowers in the garden and the impossible scent of milk mixed with honey which he always used to get stuck into. We saw his pitchfork again, his shovel and the dented metal buckets into which he used to toss the manure. We remembered his fields and his crops riddled with mildew. And had he ever experienced, we wondered, that nervous exhaustion which sends us looking for the vodka and the magic pills? Did he ever get to thinking, like us, about Saint Teresa of Àvila, whose right foot and part of her jaw are in Rome, her left hand in Lisbon, her left eye and right hand in Ronda, her left arm and heart in the reliquaries of the museum of the convent of the Annunciation in Alba de

Tormes, and her fingers somewhere else in Spain? That's what was running through our heads.

Our dismemberment.

So, we put on our face masks, took the bus, and came all the way here. With our pockets full of pumpkin seeds. Beans and potato tubers. Zinnias. Asters. Tulips and sunflowers. And Gran, we brought your grave back to life.

8

Regarding the great sequoia

Our 'spatial awareness' wasn't great, Doctor Vandenhout. The concepts of left and right have always been abstract notions to us. As a result of which we were held back another year at infant school, four years instead of three, Doctor. The price you pay for being a bit slow. Later, having passed more batteries of tests to check that all our fries had well and truly found their way into the same bag, we were able to walk in cheerful lines through the schoolyard, football club locker rooms, scout camps, amusement parks and between the dark pews of remote churches where we experienced boredom in all its immeasurable dimensions. We were children, like any others, Doctor Vandenhout. Awkward kids, sure, but considered able to cope with the practical aspects of social life. Later still, we passed other tests, obtained this or that diploma, filled out numerous forms, had numerous certificates stamped, the significance of which we never quite understood, to the point that by the end of our twenty-first year, lacking the basics (everything), we would sleep in guinea pig enclosures where scientists like you used to drug us and study us for 17 cents a night (they earned more, Doctor, obviously). At the same time, on our days off, we fell into the habit of setting the mini roosters in our alarm clocks to go off at four or five o'clock, then wandering through the down-at-heel areas where Mr Jobseeker required us to present ourselves along with our efforts to find a job but most importantly, with evidence of those attempts. Cover letters and CVs, Doctor Vandenhout. So, in those days, we would scoff left-over, ecstasy-laced pizzas on the weekend and, a hurried shower and eight RER stops later, downing our first Red Bull of the day, we would be off to conquer these interviews which were supposed to open up the glorious door to the world of work.

We no longer wanted to hear talk of any guinea pig laboratories or pharmaceutical experiments.

We were twenty-seven years old. Polite and green as young wood, Doctor, we were disheartened when we were sent on our way, but would kick off again in a flash, more motivated than ever, as soon as the verdict was handed down (the verdict was always a no). The business of being a man: that was the trade we wanted to learn. It was the only one that mattered, so we did other 'qualifying' training, to use Mr Jobseeker's words, at the same time as a bit of begging, which nobody knew about. Not our family, nor our friends. We showed willing, did everything to make ourselves more desirable in the eyes of a world that did not desire us and one into which, Doctor, forgive us for adding this, we always felt as though we had just been casually tossed.

Finally, one day, a voice answered our call. 'Come in. You have a spark of something in your eyes,' it said. A second later, we had passed through to the other side. We went about boasting, an employee's pink ID stuck to our shirt, because for the first time we were able to drink superior quality beers, eat superior quality burgers, and rest up. Everything became superior. And yet, out of habit, nostalgia, or because misfortune is a circular thing, we continued to bear the odious traces of our adolescence. Why change? We were twenty-nine years old and, every morning, we would head off to tip out sacks of plaster on our mind-numbing building sites, build towers of stone and metal, as well as fast cars the likes of which nobody had previously seen, ever. We were the ones who built things, on the bottom rung of the production line, and we'd be yelled at. We slogged away but still we were poor. Less poor than before and less poor than some others, but skint all the same. And that's when we understood that poverty, too, is a circular thing, that we were getting nowhere, regardless of what Mr Jobseeker was telling us. We were working, Doctor, but still we weren't happy.

Our happiness had been tossed to us back in our early childhood like a ball thrown to a dog at a training session, and still we were unable to find it, no matter what we did nor how much heart we put into our efforts. Worse, it rolled further and further away with every day that passed, days which, more so than if we had been asleep, seemed to go by as if we weren't even there. Without us. Which is why we continued to do what we were doing, but we went easy. Taking days to finish jobs on the site that should have taken hours.

Then we got married. They were beautiful years. Admirable children called Jasper, Ronni, Zaïda, Ashley and Marie-Thérèse. But in spite of everything, we used to drink, more and more we drank, because we were hurting, everywhere, we drank so much our belly started to resemble a keg of rum like those of our fathers, and it was then we understood that misfortune is even more circular than happiness. We took pills to help us hang in there, to sleep, pills to keep faith, to stay awake, to get hard. We were lost, Doctor. All we could feel was the uncertainty of the times. It stammered about within us. At night, it knotted itself to our breathing. And we would drink another seven or eight cans, then go upstairs to bed, more concerned about how not to wake up than how to fall asleep.

And then, one day as we were approaching our thirty-fourth birthday—good God above! Where does the time go?—the chain on the freight hoist on the site where we were rotting away got stuck in a tree. On this vast construction site, right next to the station. That's right. So we attempted to climb the tree to free the chain and, from up there—such a handsome tree, Doctor, strong, straight and welcoming, the way it bore our weight——we saw things differently.

We freed up the chain.

The freight hoist engine started up again, as did work on the site.

But stuck up there in Paradise, looking at our hands

which had just freed up the chain, we saw the whole world in a new light. The things we had made and our machines, the thousand and one projects in which our hands had been involved, all the obstacles we had overcome to get to this point, to this promotion indicated by the employee's pink ID, all of it felt unjust, undignified.

Time went by. Our co-workers, who were leaving the premises, ended up forgetting all about us. Night fell. And just as we were thinking about Italo Calvino's baron in the trees, which our teachers had been so fond of, the idea struck us that the big mistake lay in making oneself known, that in any event, it was far better not to show one's face, Doctor Vandenhout. To stop running. To stop manipulating the angry puppets that we are. To understand—to feel—the lack of logic in a world which functions with no concept of rest. That's where we had landed. We were looking at the world from the only place where our issues with spatial awareness stopped being a problem.

So the following day, we discreetly came down, discreetly climbed over the barbed wire gates, avoided the inspection points, the unmarked quad bikes of the police of the police, then made our way along the growling, thrumming motorways, and grabbing our wives and our kids, traversed troubled lands, between fallen, broken rocks, like in that Gus Van Sant film, the title of which we've forgotten. And then we climbed up here, into this great sequoia, where we're now carrying on this conversation with you.

Pointless.

We're not coming down.

What could be better than playing hide-and-seek in the branches while we wait for night to fall?

... To our children? We tell them stories from who knows where. Except for some of them, the stories which we've experienced, Doctor? About the fact that once upon a time we were happy? That, back then, joy was part of who we were?

... What stories do we tell them?

All stories are a salve. All stories heal. We tell them, whatever they may be.

The story of an old woman with lilac hair, who cuts oranges grown in the mountains and eats them, with a piece of bread spread with margarine, in a house which shakes all over.

An eighty-year-old woman who does nothing but knit babies' clothes while watching 'The Young and the Restless'.

A man who takes his bath with his eyes shut, because that way he is more intimately aware of the water's warmth.

Kids wearing straw hats in remote villages in remote worlds, who smile as they stare at the sun and imagine themselves to be elsewhere. In Sicily. In Sardinia. Somewhere like that.

A little wooden boat that travels through time.

A guy who pisses on his shoe and lets loose a stream of incoherent ravings.

The scalp of a raspberry ice cream that a kid drops into the gutter among the paper boats he made with his father which are floating away.

A wall taken over by hardy plants.

The fading summer.

An artist uncle who buries his bottles of cider in the soil of his kitchen garden which is riddled with them.

The somnolence of old trunks of toys whose keys can no longer be found.

The asthma attacks of children who were not supposed to have continued along the road of the living, but who did so, nonetheless, Doctor, notwithstanding all their issues with spatial awareness.

9

Regarding the minority who became the majority

Yesterday, we were the girls on the margins. And being marginal, our words had no price tags, and sales of our books, if they happened to sell, amounted to thirty-four copies or so. Except that they weren't even books, rather pamphlets, six or seven pages long. Lame texts to which nobody paid any attention, because the language they were written in, the barely legible language of our earlier books, was littered with asteroids. Our mothers didn't understand a word. They couldn't understand why we wrote in languages only we knew, our own sacred languages deliberately mud-flecked, our reliable old languages from caverns which nonetheless fully faced the light, because that's how we wanted it. We wanted to shine. To gather as much speed as possible sharpening our tongues on the purest of stones. And not be understood.

It was magical.

We used to recycle our pain.

We exchanged the paternal shadow for comets, lights and other asteroids. And from our mothers' retreat, we gathered the force of our momentum. In short, whoever tried to catch us, to see through us, developed chest pains.

... Our words? They stuck to our innards like the children we hadn't had. There were words everywhere, more and more of them. Nobody expected anything from us and the idea of seducing a public was such an absurd notion that it was not even contemplated.

In many ways, our writing was unwieldy.

Our words rewilded.

Reforested.

... Was anyone at the time holding out a microphone to us? But Mister Journalist, since when do the green years of youth require a microphone? What message did we have for the world that was so urgent it absolutely called for a microphone? All that was at stake we can sum with these words of Ingeborg Bachmann, whom we used to read like the possessed and whose work we loved more than ever:

I have to tell you, the word melted away
with the last snow in the garden.

Our feet are so raw from the many, many stones
One of them is healing. We want to use that one to jump
until the children's king, with the key to his kingdom
   in his mouth
fetches us, and we shall sing:

What a beautiful time it is when the date seed sprouts!
All those who fall have wings.

Don't you see? All we wanted was the intoxication and speed of the story. Words spat out like bullets from a Kalashnikov, taking us far from that other language, the one we had been taught, whose very presence had always threatened our well-being. Whenever we were around that other language, our heads had always secreted away the spores of our asthma which, from the age of ten, became our worst enemy. Ten was the age we were when we wrote our first anarchist texts and the age we suffered our first asthma attacks, when our bronchial tubes resembled a garden path strewn with dead leaves. The leaves piled up. And we lived among them. Among leaves which crushed everything, clogging the guttering of our fathers' country houses, rotting their lawn, suffocating it. We have never written in order to be loved. All we wanted was to free our body from its sex, its size, its weight, its voice, the colour of its skin, its name, all of it, and from the entirety of the burdens commonly referred to as 'attributes', provide it with a place of honesty. And it wasn't just that our language was that place, it replaced our bodies and took up all the space. So that we existed only when we were singing. How our words whistled! Such that when we looked back to uncover their meaning, we, too, had chest pains.

How quickly they flew. Far. High.

We felt these things.

The joy of a language owing nothing to anybody and to

which even we would not reply. Freedom!

A language of hunters and huntresses of maggots and masticaters of marl.

At fifteen, it changed. We had so blackened the pages of our notebooks that our words became transparent . . . Like trout seen through the water of a pond, if you like, yes, Mister Journalist. We saw them dancing and flipping their tails, shifting in the weed. They had lived in darkness for so long that they had grown accustomed to it, felt at home there. By the way, that was when we started signing our poems. Until that point, our language had categorically resisted it. But from the age of fifteen onwards, even our most negligible output (a word which itself resists categories) received the seal of ownership. Similarly, we started to see some recurrent themes bloom on the surface of our poems. The fact of having been assaulted (the noted paternal shadow). The fact of being angered by the idea of growing up in this mindless world. The fact of not managing to portray ourselves better, of feeling that we were floating, our edges blurred. Others felt compelled to fight, and that, too, became a recurrent theme.

Put another way, our words had become legible.

At twenty-five, the more mature among us gave their first interviews. And you remember: that was you at the other end of the boom, because you weren't yet posing the questions, you were the aspiring poser of questions. At the same time, some were forming a desire to write a novel. They were obsessed. Poetry no longer sufficed. They had to move on to the novel, to the clarity of prose. And that was how suddenly voices rose up denouncing the violence of their fathers, their childhood spent in darkened chicken coops, and how long accounts of events which had, until then, remained under cover of silence, saw the light of day. We, too, came to the novel and people immediately started to read us, and the press to talk about us, and we saw our faces on the news, 'The sensation of this year's literary season!' 'The event of the season!' It was true. Our thirty-four copies had multiplied one hundredfold, a thousandfold, and we'll stop there, Mister Jean from 'The Gazette'. Of course, we had signed with large publishing houses. So that it wasn't just our life which altered, but reality itself. Now we were more real than others, because 'only that which is chosen is real', as our publicists used to enjoy saying, repeating the words of our agents. 'Ingeborg Bachmann's poems? Nobody knows them, so they don't exist.' They used to say that to help us. 'That which finds an audience exists, that which fails to do so, does not.' Wherein you can clearly recognise the tautological nature of success (the only thing that works is what works), but we played the game. Full stop.

When we gave interviews, poetry never featured. And when we took off a little, our poetry was nothing less than the poetry of public speakers. Deep down, we wanted to be read, Mister Journalist. Wanted to be loved. We swore by that and that alone, and en masse disavowed our first engagements. Those who fall have wings. Do we really need a whole poem to express that? The people who read us wanted to grasp what they were reading. 'A fine novel.' 'An ode to freedom.' 'Deeply affecting.' As for you, you were gloating.

Books that are committed, with universal themes, which are read to the sound of a 'little music in your head'. That's what you wanted. And thinking that we owed you clarity, we played our parts to the point of caricature. Well, so be it. We had understood that in order to be loved, we had to deliver clear messages and become spokespeople for causes with which others could identify. We had to speak of our orphan diseases, of the rod our mothers placed on our back one day to bring us into line and make us stand up straight, and then there was the cigarette butt which, after our fathers had stuffed it up our nose, gave us cacosmia. We had to say all that, but as if 'that' could happen to anybody, or better still, that it had already happened to everybody, without anybody remembering, or having dared to say it, until we did.

We were thirty years old. We were successful and unequalled when it came to answering Proust's little questionnaire, talking about our favourite things or offering God knows what advice in the pages folles of magazines. Writing advice. Health advice. We sought out your microphones. It was all we wanted. To occupy space. For the ant to become a dragon and for the margins to become large, to take up a page.

It's over.

We've spent too much time in the limelight. So much time that our words have become slogans. Our anger has become a slogan. Our readability has gotten the better of us. As a result of our success, we've became the women who write such and such a type of book, hyena-chicks denouncing violent fathers, girls singing for the right to free themselves from old cigarette stubs, and we can't bear it anymore.

That's why we're here. We're throwing in the towel, Mister Editor in Chief, Mister Former Boom Operator, Mister Official Journalist, Mister Columnist, Mister Host of Cultural Programs, Mister Host of Comedy Shows, Mister Hater of Poetry, Mister Friend of Human Interest Stories, Mister Writer in his Spare Time. To begin with, there was only one thing we wanted to do. You can believe it or not. You'll write about it or not. Do you want us to tell you? To fill each word with our entire body, by which we mean, both the absence of our body and its infinite presence.

A free body is an impersonal body.

When we were very little, we couldn't bear the idea of being put into a box. We wanted to be multiple, incendiary, violent, unpredictable, improbable. To get into guys. And girls. We wanted hair like straw, that was all over the place, and we wanted to belch, feeling like we were powerful and important, but no more and no less than the water in the pond or the rushing stream. And, to do that, we needed to change shape, and not just our shape, but change our weapons, our songs, our cries. We had one hundred voices. One hundred thousand of them. And what remains of them?

We will no longer be binary.

Neither girls nor boys.

But both.

Girls and boys.

And, at the same time, neither.

We will be something other. Otherly.

Binary logic, oppositions, have destroyed everything,

down to the salt of the earth. Now if salt loses its taste, what does one use to bring it back? Don't try to reach us anymore. Don't speak to us anymore. Don't call us. This is where life is. In the contradiction. In the constant transformation. The worst? The worst would be to ask us to sign books written in the same words as yours. The same as those which used to clog up our fathers' guttering and give us asthma. But that won't be happening anymore. We're going back into hiding, Mister Journalist.

Here's to chest pains! To asthma! To Ingeborg Bachmann and to poetry!

10

Regarding a pain with no name

Dear husbands, this is a letter. We're writing it from our bed. Quickly, because we don't have much time. A light is calling us, not far from the starry sky, but we don't want it, not yet, not the sky, nor the stars.

It's curious.

When you have laid us in the earth, you'll be left alone with the children. Will everything be alright? . . . Do you swear? We'll be fine. Everything has become so dark, hasn't it? We believe we got it all wrong, our generation of thirty- and forty-year-olds. We had families too early, too young, and we never found ourselves again. That's what we think. We worked like dogs to earn next to nothing. We gave it our all.

But it was something else that made us sick. Our childhood. And the way it collided with the world that came afterwards.

We weren't well-to-do, yet we wanted for nothing. Really, we were lucky to grow up surrounded by 'beautiful' things (antique furniture, fine cakes and pastries, Impressionist paintings and the scent of cigarillos) which always made us feel overcome with nostalgia since, as adults, we have not managed to bring all that back.

We wanted to be the same as our parents, to do the same as they had. To prosper. But we were short of money and then we wanted it all, everything and its opposite.

To live in the city and in the country. Do you remember? Everything. We wanted everything and its opposite. We dreamed about VW Californias, camper-vans and great big vehicles beyond our price range which would take us deep into the woods and return us to the wilderness. There was no question, we were missing some savagery in our lives. Did we do the right thing, having children? Of course. Even if we've come to the view, each in our own way these last years, that we no longer want to live together. Something between us was no longer working, notwithstanding our immense love.

But we held on.

You in the little cabin.

Us in the little conservatory.

There was no 'custody calendar' setting out the days we would be obliged to see our children, nor the amount of fees we were supposed to pay for their education.

We were separated, but together.

We didn't have to get drunk to grow used to the children's absence, to be able to bear it, like some many of our girlfriends had to do, and still do. We got drunk from despair, because the world was making us ill. Miserable and ill. And here we are again. With our much talked-about pains. Our fibromyalgia. Our chronic fatigue syndrome. Our inability to grasp what was nonetheless beckoning us, like that light. Not yet. We love you. We haven't finished.

For us, it was the pain which made us, that was the thing which always nailed us together, as if to the cross. Without the pain, we were nothing. Let's just say it. Because of the state of the world, our eyes are ringed with black, our nights have become electric chairs, life has become a three-laned highway for the traffic of our fears. Wherever one goes, sadness works its way in. We were replete with happiness, before. Over time, it has soured.

We're going to tell you something else.

The other day, summoning the strength to go out, we found ourselves some little pellet air guns which had come from the rifle shop—you know, next to the garden with the fake oranges. For once in our life, we wanted to show off. But, more than anything, we wanted to shoot into the crowd and for people to run for their lives, to flee. That's what we wanted, and we are not ashamed, because we needed some space in the middle of the crush of people and the commotion. But do you know what? Sputtering badly, our poor air guns only let out three or four miserable 'ploofs', and no pellets. Not a single one.

In other words: even when we want to attack, when we want to do some damage, it's a failure. Why? Because, just as we are doomed to suffer, we are also doomed to do the right thing. Our whole education has been based on that, on dreary, inoffensive little 'ploofs'. Do you see what I'm saying?

That's why we fell ill. And there you were, copping it, with all our children. While we were lying down, destroyed, in the little conservatory, unable to work, and cursing our beloved parents for the good fortune, the lack of concern and the security they had enjoyed.

Their houses, the stupid names they gave to their stupid dogs, which began replacing us over the course of the months and years while their cars became ever bigger at the end of the garden path.

You, too, with your preoccupations, you were envious of the price they had paid for their house (Oh! That garden! Oh! Those trees!), the way they were calm, the trips they enjoyed, their honeymoon in India, another one in Acapulco, their new television. We envied it all. Even the way they would go to church without questioning a thing. The way they believed in God and how they voted, believed in God just as they voted, in fact, without any particular conviction, and less out of habit than of torpor. And where are their excuses now? Will they be rolled out?

For a long time, we went to their place wanting to have a go at them for it all but, not having the guts, we fell ill, like Sylvia Plath, like Fritz Zorn, and so many other crackpots. It was just that we had to be good. Be proper, so as not to disappoint them. Look happy, including the times when we were scavenging like hungry dogs in the gutters of misfortune. Behave ourselves. Have a good job (even though we were scraping the bottom of the barrel), goals, a healthy lifestyle, decent values, appropriate attentiveness, a fitting sense of humour. When in fact, in our heads it was carnage.

We weren't sure of anything. Not even our breathing.

And once we were back home, we would dissolve into tears and curse ourselves, having so dreamed about speaking to them. So they could know, for example, that the day they retired and cracked open a jeroboam in front of their mates, that their grandchildren had eaten their own nail clippings at dinner. But instead of which, we swallowed our saliva, because we were the sweetest of sweet, and the kindest of kind. What do you do? While the notion of suffering was no secret to us, sadism, on the other hand, remained an unknown. Masochism, however, was a sensation that was never far away. For we would return, week after week, to say hello, dying of hunger . . . What did we want? For them to tell us they loved us. Did they? No. But we kept returning to the site of our own crucifixion. To no other end but exhaustion. With no other possibility of stopping except a breakdown. Since that was the life we were leading . . . Yes, you may. You may sit down next to us. But promise that tomorrow you'll take the children far away. Don't show them the grave, or anything else. Leave. Go deep into the night. Ever further . . . Take the caravan, yes, the one with all the dents on the side. Drive. And when the world shows you its least appealing face, stop and settle down. But remember that where you stop, there'll be no more Christmas trees, and anything that bears any resemblance to any celebrations will have to be banned. In addition, because one can feel nostalgic about the slightest thing, and it's best to be exhaustive, all memories of birthday celebrations, communions, weddings, excursions, holidays and water fights in the amusement park, reminiscing and smiling will also be banned. Don't take any books or photographs that bear any relation to the old days. Promise! Prepare the little ones to fight. That's what we missed out on. An outward-facing rage. Make sure they have in the place of hands neither our piercings, nor our 'ploofs', nor our excuses. In their heads, neither our indecisions nor our fear. Get ahead of the game if you want them to have an effective education. Something that's useless now, won't be tomorrow, much like something that was indispensable yesterday might turn out to be toxic today. The same might be said about our education, perfect, certainly, for the times, but disastrous in this loveless world. The little girls we once were, with our sacrosanct humilities, our attentiveness, none of it has any currency any longer, moreover it has turned against us. Consumed us. Do it, won't you? Train them. Make sure they learn how to sing in the midst of bomb-blasted concrete, under meteor showers, make sure they know to make a fire from their tears, how to get by with three screws and two pieces of dowel found lying around on the ground to build machines, two cents and some old rags roughly knitted together to guard against the frost. Like in Cormac McCarthy's The Road. Let them kill and avenge their mothers with their damaged nerves. Similarly, let them pray to the god of rivers and red moons, while remaining ready for the time when, in a world in which wealth and poverty have ceased to exist, the only meaningful justice will consist of holding strong in battle, in the forests, or what will remain of them, in the fields, or what will remain of them, while drinking in long-forgotten caverns and hewing stones.

Hunting. Biting. Gentle no more. Gentle no more.

11

Regarding a recovered distant joy

That day, we turned out the lights and left.

It was at the time we were working as stock controllers for one of the three big chains in the country. Stock controllers. No longer pianists, sculptors, writers. The State could no longer abide the noise of our pens and our notorious 'stances', to use their words. They muddled people's thoughts. They served no purpose.

Let's clarify that the crisis had been raging for months and, as everybody knows, our President was not making any more concessions. The time for half-measures was over. People had to roll up their sleeves, find real jobs and kick-start the economy once and for all, that's what he'd bellow during the traditional one-minute-long, televised Presidential evening address. Which is how, contrary to the ordinary course of things, and to our health, we became stock controllers. Instruments of the State. Under the State's conditions. Every day, we arranged earthenware jars of red lentils along the bottom shelves, fair-trade bananas in fake cane baskets and seitan juice in cheap and nasty demijohn bottles. An uninterrupted chain of actions which found neither their beginning nor their end with us. Luckily, we had stopped thinking. Pamphlets and diatribes, Bach partitas which had been our whole lives, poems which had rescued us so many years previously, sculptures not made from clay but from apple or cherry wood, how long ago it all seemed, how we had grown oblivious! All that remained were earthenware jars of red lentils and fair trade nosh, wherever we looked.

Our children thought we were brave. Because with our salary, we had just enough to buy our own lentils, and craft beers plus a few bananas that were more or less fair trade. Enough to pay the rent and pay for those bits and pieces flogged to us as 'happiness'. We no longer went away on holidays. Our cars had been turned into soap box racers. Overgrown with creepers that had made their way into the engines. Our wives, for their part, were selling swimsuits and inflatable swimming pools in other large chain stores. Sunscreen and tweezers. Floaties and cheap bangles . . . In that part of town where all the barbers are, yes, not far from the main square and the statue of the President. We had the shirt on our backs and 1,350 euros a month. Let me say that again: 1,350 euros. 600 euros for our wives, 750 for us. What did we have to complain about?

We no longer watched television. We looked at other screens, but without knowing what we were looking at. We were done in. Nailed to the spot by exhaustion. In order to save, we started to eat black market seitan and poorer quality chickpeas. 'For you who produce everything and who have nothing but what is left to you by those who produce nothing and yet have everything.' That is how we swallowed it, singing along with Kropotkin.

On some evenings, our children demanded that we play them a little Verdi, those were their words, 'Papa, mama, if you don't play us a little Verdi we won't go up to bed!' So we did as they said, tapping it out on our thighs (we had sold the piano) and our wives singing along painfully, as if singing was the manifestation of a circular saw turning deep within them. Their singing was so beautiful, so sad.

The day they fell ill, we carried on. Every day. Leaped into our soap box racers as if nothing was wrong. Off to the shop, did our jobs, didn't think too much. Our bosses never knew our wives were in such terrible pain, their whole body suffering. Pain nobody could ever put a name on. Suffering until their death.

They died without anybody being able to put a name to it. A Friday. Gone, flown away forever.

On the day of the funeral, the State had a bouquet of organic tulips delivered to us, grown in the Saint-Remacle fens, a few kilometres away from our place. Then they issued a bill, for that same bouquet of organic tulips. What did we have to complain about? Hadn't we received a bunch of organic tulips? Was it not a consoling gesture? Well, then?

Our children used to play in the cemetery, among the wild flowers and the plastic bouquets. So little and so grown up.

We, however, had to pay for their school, pay for the heating oil.

As a result, the beer started to flow freely.

Our bosses told us off because of it. We were a sorry sight, worse than pigs, they said. We were drinking too much.

That lasted eight weeks.

Then we started suffering our wives' pains. Once again, some nameless pain. The doctors, guessing we were seriously depressed, prescribed us enough happy pills for a horse. Their preferred treatment. But the void, the vertigo, the fear, they just kept growing. And when the pain went away, it didn't go far. It crushed our bones. It became harder and harder to breathe.

To the point that one morning in March, we turned off the lights and closed the door behind us. Put the key under the pot of geraniums, the national flower of our heavenly country, then sprinkled pumpkin seeds and tomato seeds on the graves of our wives. We left a note for our children under the geranium pot, too. *Make the best of it.* Signed: *Papa.* And taking almost nothing with us, we started to jog. First down the lane, then along the main road, and then up into the mountains, into Graciano's deep, blue forests. Along the streams. We jogged. As gently and with as much sadness as the loves of our lives when they used to sing. We stopped only to eat. The cold made life hard, but to the extent it crushed the pain within it brought some healing. And we would think about our little ones, along with all we had lost. And we kept moving forward.

Up well before dawn, we slipped along as if over a frozen body of water, listening to noises carried to us by invisible forms and then we would run on in peace, in the dark, listening to the murmuring, cracking stones, scaling rocks from which we would then hurtle down, cooling off in pools and mountain streams. We had no possessions. A little bit of food, a flask of water. We hated shorts, but our legs were naked, because nothing made us feel more alive than exposing them to nature's whipping. That's where we lived and what we became, little by little. Artists turned long distance runners. Caught in the thorns and glaciers, our legs ruined by cold, listening out for the birds.

What if blisters make the soles of our feet burn? We bury them in the soil and eat the tips of sprouting acorns; we love their scarlet colour. We're no longer able to leave the woods, nor stop running.

Like our hero, Anton Krupicka.

Like before.

When we used to find happiness not in our feet but in our music, our voices and our minds that were poor but free.

Like the time when the women in our lives were by our sides. When our nights weren't electric chairs of anxiety, but a sumptuous respite punctuated with mouthfuls of wine and sinuous moaning. Nothing is lost. As long as we keep running, they keep watch over us. They wait for daybreak. They take our hand and, armed with the fishing net they have always used to settle upon us, the great net of their gentleness, they send us back out onto the trails, while we dream of one thing only: to feel for one last time the molten animal of their mouth, so that it can nourish us with the scent of mulberries and milk which it always used to leave on our skin. Then we get back to it. Slopes, hills, streams.

We tear down them. When cars brush past us, no stress. Because we are tough men. But it does, nonetheless, make us think back to when we were stuck in our soap boxes in the traffic. For 750 euros a month, we got to shuffle along in traffic jams! A world supposed to move faster and faster but only getting slower. Energy fit to burst, but increasingly muzzled. A world of infinite solitudes, ever more alone and divided by the power and impotence of money. All those objects, all those gifts we no longer wanted to hear about, but which continued to be distributed to the four winds of our contradictions. Now, the wind is our guide. We have our tempo. Our steps dictated by the pinching of our lips, like the song of an Armenian duduk: it's all we have left. We smile, thinking about Christmas approaching and how we'd like to gift our children hours of silence, and kilos of nothing, and kilometres of unspoiled time and holidays on mountain tops. With us. A Christmas with no gift wrapping. Like before, when our biggest luxury was to run, to jump and to throw. Explosion and passion. When we were swift and had no expectations, when we knew nothing but so many things were hatching within us. A time when knowledge was gleaned through one's feet. When, as we moved, we understood about the creatures that had lived in these parts, five hundred thousand years earlier. When, hidden in the midst of all this, in low, thick, dense vegetation, we understood about the men, our ancestors, armed with pikes and lances with sharpened tips, gathering, hunting and living in those caves where what belonged to one belonged also to others. Surrounded by stupendous nature. That's what we want their Christmas presents to be. The intensity of something too full of life to worry about leaving a trace.

And, closing our eyes, we dream of the day when instead of this endless proliferation, there will instead be ministers for mountain tracks, ministers for pretty streets and for their beautification, ministers for skateboards, for woodpiles, for haystacks, ministers for siestas for all, ministers for forgiveness and trail running sneakers, ministers for memories, for old age and for time that passes, ministers for dogs, for beetles, ministers for listening to the earth, to the water, to the wind, to the weak and to the vulnerable. Ministers for the importance of dreaming, of music and of words. And, with that, we will carry on our way.

12

Regarding some questions

One day we saw the light. Now, it's night-time. Where does it go, the light, when you can no longer see it? Is it possible the light remains hidden somewhere, suspended, beyond reach? Like the final note of a song which continues to resonate after everything else has fallen silent? Or is it like the voice of the dead? Once it has gone, Mister President, does something which used to shine continue to exist in some other form? In other colours? Where does the light go? What does it become when it flees time and our sight? And since we must accept that there was, once, some light, acknowledging that our skin is baked and tanned all over, we wonder: how, why did we not cherish it? As a result of what? Why did we not watch over it? How did we not see it go out? Or, at least, how did we agree to acknowledge it was going out? . . . Don't answer. Shush. We have other things to say. More questions. Later, you can answer later . . . What other questions? Three billion, Mister President, because there are three billion of us, three billion people in a torpor, their voices muffled by their mask. Shush. These are not just words, Mister President, our questions are real. We hurl them into the shadows with the strength of those who hope for nothing but expect everything. We want them to go to the very heart of the matter, and make burgeoning buds of our pain. We express them in words, yet they are neither slogans nor speeches. But our nerves, our sleepless nights, our health which has been destroyed along with our inability to say the word 'future' without bursting into laughter, Mister President. Tell us. Teach us how to say the word 'future' without bursting into laughter . . . Shush. We're not saying we don't like you, but your cookie-cutter slogans, your 'on the spot' answers, your bogus undertakings . . . To think that we did love you, yesterday. You had our trust. We gave it to you unquestioningly . . . Who are we to speak like this? We are the ones who no longer sleep, unlike you, who need only three hours a night, you say, something you gloat about.

Another question for you: do you know why we'd like to sleep? . . . Ha ha! Not at all! No, Mister President, that has absolutely nothing to do with it! Completely beside the point! We're not interested in work. Nobody believes in it anymore, apart from you. It's a wall-eyed chimera. No, we'd like to sleep in order to access the stuff of our dreams, their fullness. To remain surrounded by blurred images and thoughts owing nothing to anybody but ourselves, that's what we want . . . Are we waxing lyrical? Yes, but it's the lack of sleep which is behind that. The lack of sleep is our inspiration. You know that better than anybody: lyricism is a saving grace. Hence our question: how is it we are not yet dead? How is it that we have not given up? That we are here speaking to you, hoping to relaunch our dreams, instead of having been laid to eternal rest, huh? On the other hand—shush, we're the ones speaking—how is it that we were thinking about our life and liberties as if they were distant notions that will never come back, Mister President of the Shadows? Our youth was dead before it even made an appearance. We were eighteen years old, then we were twenty, twenty-three, twenty-six, and now here we are, adrift, between the world of our childhood and that of adulthood, each one clashing with the other. Each of them like lost continents. What fools we are! The beers we used to drink on café terraces as soon as the weather turned for the better, the first time we kissed a boy's breast, the first time we camped out in the wilderness, far from our parents, ten of us sharing the same tent, the same vapours from the Moroccan dope, we're nostalgic for it, all of it, like the last strawberry of the season or the taste of the last cherry, if you see what we're getting at. And also, why do we already talk about the 'olden days' when we're just talking about yesterday? Is our fate already sealed? . . . Go take a leak, sure. But don't forget to do up your fly. You always forget your fly, Mister President . . . You're done already? . . . You're going to have to leave us? You've run out of time? The electoral campaign is well under way? But what is time, in a world with no light, what even is it? Does it exist? Will there still be any tomorrow? For what? Time and light: and what if they were one and the same thing, we ask, You-Who-Are-Responsible for our madness? What if light were the tangible face of time, its caress? And what if there were no more light, where does time go then? Where is it hiding? And what do we do?

Teach us how to breathe in tempo.

Tell us how not to die of laughter when we talk about it, when we talk of the future... Sure. It's not just you and your conjuring tricks that have brought us to this point. We're in it too. We believed in you and we were wrong. We are reaping our negligence, that is all. But all the same. There used to be light and now there is none. Good night. And you did nothing. You watched the day slip away as if over a beach in the Balearics, sipping the Spritz of the blessed in the company of friends. Those with a VIP pass. A syrupy wind was blowing. You were happy. So you took off your swimsuit and dived into the sea, where you swam, followed by the mermaids and silverfish of your security detail. Then you opened your eyes again and, putting your suit back on, you did the job. Saying and promising things you weren't doing and would never do, on the one hand, and on the other, taking on other things which you didn't talk about and would no longer talk about. In a way which meant that the light didn't just dwindle all at once, but in successive waves, to match your betrayals and, let's admit it, our propensity for denial... Of course. Everything we're saying is being recorded. We are the hollow men, we need evidence. Fractured, schizophrenic beneath our raincoats, we no longer know which way to turn our head. Too many realities, opinions, details, and at the same time, nothing more at all, as if everything had been emptied out.

The generation who wants to fight, who should be finding work, except that there is none, the generation who isn't interested in growth, who wants to leave the world of money behind, rely less on it, yet not want for it, the generation of cabin-builders, incapable of using a hammer without bashing a nail into a finger.

Hence our state of shock.

Can we continue to hold out? No. Will we hold out? Yes. Because we are the champions of contradiction, our whole lives are a contradiction. And, whether we like it or not, our favourite sport is very similar to yours: not doing what we said we would and promising what we won't do. We're torn. Our actions on the right flank, our impotence on the other. Advance, retreat, to the left, to the right . . .

And what about you? How do you do it? Put on your underpants every morning, brush your teeth. How do you do it?

There's more. If we had agreed to watch the dying of the light, rather than just close our eyes, where would we be? Isn't that what ruined everything? Thinking that the clarity would last because we were so beside ourselves about it fading? Dying from having wanted to live at all costs? From constantly having wanted more? What if the light were only to last provided we reconciled ourselves to the fact we might lose it?

Hello. We're over here. Stupid and with no future, because we're young, but with a truth in our bellies that no stake, no militia, no law enforcement will prevent us expressing: the certainty that the point at which your systems, your speed, your societies, your technologies, are most highly developed is precisely that point at which it becomes a vicious circle, the snake biting its tail . . . Shush. You talk all the time, every day it's the same. We watch you, you know. You talk and talk, like a little kid, whistling as though that will humanise even your treachery. 'What's he saying now, the fool?' shouts our mum from the sofa, at the window looking onto the park where the homeless are. 'Nothing!' bellows the old man, for whom every one of your appearances could be a crucifixion. 'Nothing new, Gertrude, nothing special.' Yes, You-Who-Are-Responsible for our being locked up, Minister Keeper-of-the-Keys to the museum of our contradictions, our mothers are called Gertrude and our fathers, Désiré. We're not making it up. Much like you, who lies as you seek to reassure us, and reassures us as you lie. But we're grown now. We actually live in the real world. That's not what's killing us, it's your trickery. Speak to us like adults. Thank you. Proud, fighting women. Upstanding men. Neither idiots nor crooks. Tenderly. Tell us why our voices to you are so distant, and what it is you are planning to do to address this expanding desert between your world and ours. Tell us what to expect and where this bewilderment is coming from. Do it tenderly. Come on. As you would to a brother. Explain to us what happens next. What would happen, for example, if one day we all fell asleep at the same time, Mister President, humans and objects? Or if, in some desperately undreamed moment, we managed to do the opposite, to wake up completely, all of us together. Tell us, then what.

Principal guides to the museum

Roland Barthes (quoted in Philippe Sollers' *Agent secret*), Yevgeny Zamyatin and his novel, *We*, Italo Calvino's *The Baron in the Trees*, "*The Game is Over*" by Ingeborg Bachmann, the poetry of Sylvia Plath, the poetry of Roberto Juarroz, Fritz Zorn and his novel, *Mars*, the books of Marc Graciano, Verdi (everything), F. Scott Fitzgerald, Pier Paolo Pasolini and his *Corsair Writings*, Cormac McCarthy's *The Road*, Nénène, Mémé, Pépé and Papou, Félix, Victor, Sélim and Delia, Violette Leduc (*Je hais les dormeurs*), Gus Van Sant's "Gerry", and ultra-runner, Anton Krupicka.

Translator's note

I would like to thank Passa Porta, Belgium, for the invaluable opportunity to attend the 2024 "Seneffe in August" literary residency where I enjoyed the generous support of fellow authors and translators in my work on this translation.

Stephanie Smee, Sydney, June 2025